Dexter, 7, Hockey Player

Sophia, 9, Doctor

Brennan, 7, Basketball Player

Julia, 10, Illustrator

Ava, 7, Nurse

Lara, 7, Artist

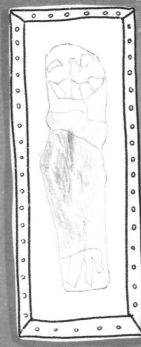

Joseph, 10, Footballer

Mailey, 8, Pediatrician

Jonah, 4, Doctor

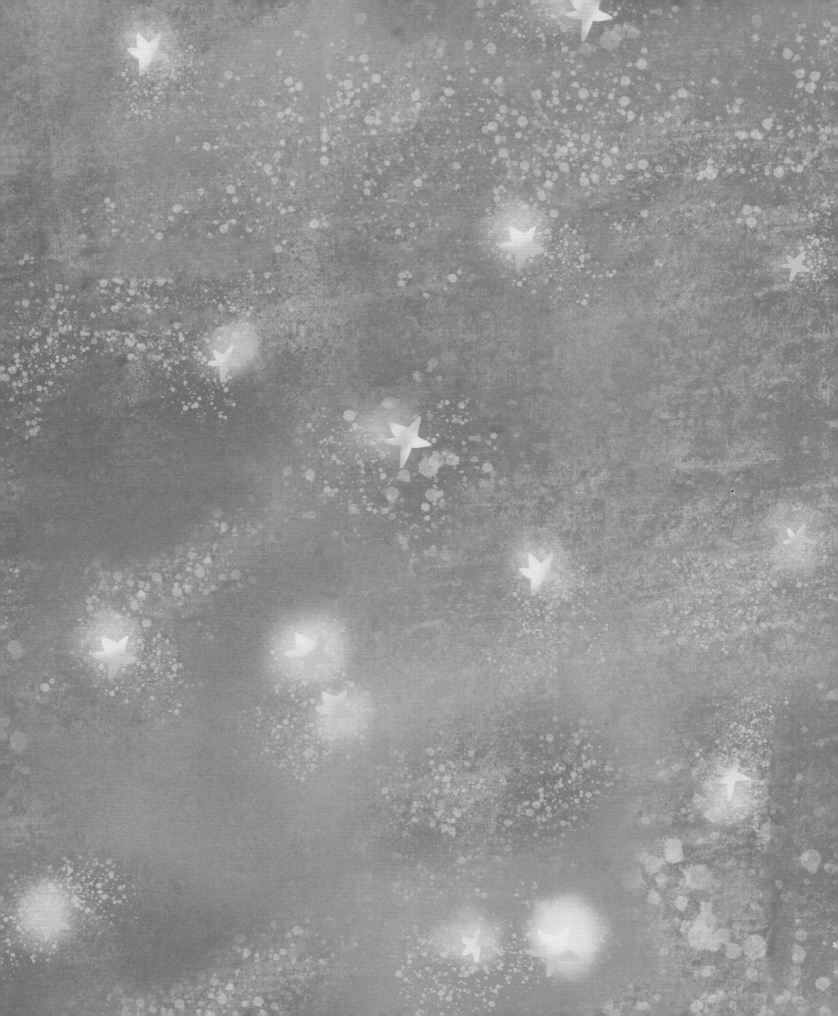

This could be You

Be Brave! Be True! Believe! Be You!

By Cindy Williams Schrauben

Illustrated by Julia Seal

This Could be You

Summary: Will you be an astronaut? Farmer? An artist? A nurse? No matter where your dreams take you, your own unique flair will get you there. Keep pushing...it could be you!

Our books may be purchased in bulk for promotional, educational or business use. Please contact your local bookseller.

Library of Congress Control Number: 2021936495
ISBN (hardcover): 978-1-7353451-3-0
ISBN (Ebook): 978-1-7353451-4-7

The art in this book was created using Procreate

Book design by: Maggie Villaume

Cardinal Rule Press

5449 Sylvia
Dearborn Heights, MI 48125
Visit us at www.CardinalRulePress.com

Before Reading

- Look at the cover of the book and the title. What do you think this book will be about?

- You can be anything when you grow up! What would you like to be?

- To become what you want to be, what do you think is important to learn?

While Reading

- Is there a main character in this book? (no)

- Does this book have a setting? (several) Name a few!

- What is the message the author is trying to share with you?

After Reading

- Go back to a page that you liked and tell me why.

- Can you find a page where a child had to try something several times before getting it right?

- Learning new things may get hard. What should you do if they do?

Dedications

To Mom, Dad,
Doug, Sam, and Hannah...
for encouraging me to
believe in my dreams.
**- Cindy Williams
Schrauben**

For Joseph and
Amalie
- Julia Seal

Who pursues their **top** dreams,

their **never-ever-stop** dreams,

persist-until-they-drop dreams?

Believe. It could be you!

Who displays **explore** drive,

an astronaut's **let's-soar** drive,

a **faster-higher-more** drive?

Blast off. It could be you!

Who has **keen-design** flair,

an artist's **time-to-shine** flair,

a **sketch-and-then-refine** flair?

Create. It could be you!

Who inspires **team**work,

an athlete's **go-full-steam** work,

the **fight-to-reign-supreme** work?

Play on. It could be you!

Who has **dig-by-hand** grit,

a farmer's **rain-is-grand** grit,

a **please-respect-the-land** grit?

Plow through. It could be you.

Who completes the **long** haul,

a trucker's **staying-strong** haul,

a **fixing-what-is-wrong** haul?

Roll on. It could be you!

Who extends a **care** touch,

a nurse's **always-there** touch,

a **hopeful-don't-despair** touch?

Support. It could be you.

Who observes with **pro** eyes,

a scientist's **go-slow** eyes,

the **always-more-to-know** eyes?

Inspect. It could be you!

Who maintains a **brave** face,

a captain's **never-cave** face,

it's-rough, but-ride-the-wave face?

Jump in. It could be you!

Who selects the **right** words,
an author's **let's-unite** words,
intrigue-inform-incite words?

Compose. It could be you!

Who dares **off-the-cuff** feats,
a firefighter's **rough** feats,
the **vow-to-do-enough** feats?
Protect. It could be you!

Who applies a **try** mind,

an engineer's **ask-why** mind,

an **always-aiming-high** mind?

Invent. It could be you!

Who applauds a **bold** voice,

a judge's **truth-be-told** voice,

a **right-for-young-and-old** voice?

Speak up. It could be you.

KEEP OUR
WATERS CLEAN

Who defines a **kind** view,

a teacher's **stretch-your-mind** view,

a **no-one-left-behind** view?

Instruct. It could be you.

Who believes in **your** dreams,

courageous-to-the-core dreams,

the **better-than-before** dreams?

Guess what? That who is YOU!

This could be YOU encourages a growth mindset (as opposed to a fixed mindset) which involves being flexible in the way we see the world and our abilities. Research shows that these principles help individuals (adults and children alike) to develop more resilience and a more positive belief system.

Explain the concept of a fixed (left column) vs. a growth mindset (right column) with the following examples:

Instead of saying...   Try saying...

I can't do that. . . . . I can't do that YET, but I'll keep trying.

This is too hard. . . . . . I love challenges. It will be fun to figure it out.

I failed. . . . . Mistakes are good. They help me learn.

I am bad at math. . . . . I can train my brain.

That wasn't good enough. . . . . How can I do better?

I'm bored. I'll try something new.

Ask children to listen and look for examples of a growth mindset.

Read the whole book, letting children enjoy the characters and their experiences.

Review individual pages, encouraging children to identify the character's growth mindset traits and find those attributes in themselves. You can extend their thinking by asking questions such as:

- How did these characters prove that they have a growth mindset?

- What would these characters have done if they had a fixed mindset?

- When have you maintained a **brave** face, a captain's **ride the wave** face, **set sail instead of cave** face?

- How can you define a **kind** view, a teacher's **stretch-your-mind view**, a **no-one-left-behind view**?

Don't forget to let children lead the discussion, as well. You might be surprised where the conversation goes.

Cindy Williams Schrauben

Cindy Williams Schrauben lives in Michigan where she writes books for kids that range from the truly serious to the seriously silly. Before embarking on this path, Cindy held positions as a teacher, administrator, and assistant director of a children's museum -- always striving to empower kids. She loves sharing the message that 'It's never too late to dream!' What's next? Illustrating her own picture books.

When not writing, working with other authors, or honing her craft, Cindy might be found dissecting her grandsons' shenanigans for story ideas, reading on the floor in the bookstore, or eating ice cream... ideally all at once. Learn more at www.cindyschrauben.com.

Julia Seal

Julia Seal knew from the age of five what she wanted to do for a living—draw pictures! After graduating with a degree in Graphic Design and then working in the greeting card industry (and getting covered in glitter every day!) she finally moved onto her dream job, illustrating children's books. She lives in a small village in England with her husband and two children, who provide plenty of inspiration!

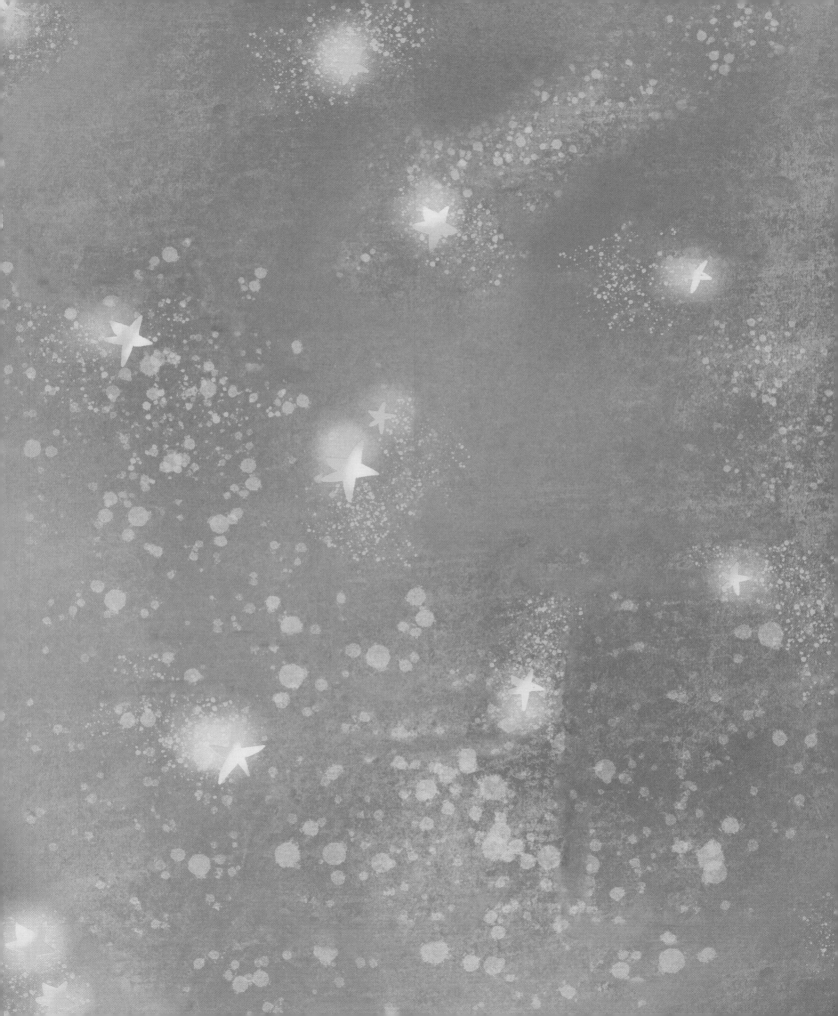

Luka, 6, Artist

Alicia, 9, Artist

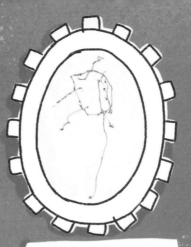

Megan, 3, Singer

Zac, 7, Football Player

Leif, 7, Animal Explorer

Athena, 10, Programmer

Aviana, 8, Teacher

Isla, 9, Musician

Katie, 8, Teacher

Leo, 4, Kitty Adopter